Gengoroh and the Thunder God

by Miyoko Matsutani   illustrated by Yasuo Segawa

English version by Alvin Tresselt

This book was translated from *Ten-ni Nobotta Gengoroh*, originally published by Kaisei Sha Publishing Company, Tokyo, Japan. The American edition has been arranged through Nippon Shuppan Hanbai K.K., Tokyo.

Parents' Magazine Press·New York

In a time before the days of our grandfathers
there lived a young man by the name of Gengoroh.
He was handsome and carefree, but seldom was
there the sound of coins jingling in his pocket;
that's how poor he was.

One day, as he strolled by the riverbank, wondering
where his next meal was coming from, he spied a
small drum hidden in the bushes.
Now this drum possessed a strange
magic, but it didn't take a clever
fellow like Gengoroh long to discover
it. If he beat lightly on one side and
said, *Nose, nose, grow long, grow
long. Bang, bang, bang,* it would
cause that very thing to happen.
If he tapped the drum on the other
side, all the time saying, *Nose, nose,
grow short, grow short. Bang, bang,
bang,* his nose would return to its
proper size.

Having learned the trick of the drum, Gengoroh ran quickly to the home of his friend, Muri.

"Look, look!" he cried. "See what I can do with this magic drum!" He beat the drum and said, *Nose, nose, grow long, grow long. Bang, bang, bang,* and his nose grew to a remarkable length right before the eyes of his startled friend. Then, just as easily, he beat on the other side and said, *Nose, nose, grow short. Bang, bang, bang,* and once more his nose was as before.

"Come with me," said Gengoroh. "We will travel from village to village. I think there may be many foolish people who will pay money to see us perform such a trick. In this way we will be able to earn a living for ourselves."

So off they went together, and it turned out just as Gengoroh
had said it would. The simple peasants were happy to part
with a few coins just to watch this remarkable thing happen.
One day, as the friends rested in the garden of a temple, they
saw a beautiful girl coming to offer her prayers.

Learning that she was the daughter of a wealthy merchant and
was about to be married, Gengoroh decided to play a trick on
her. "This may yet earn us a life of ease," he told his friend.
He tapped the drum and said, *The nose of the girl will grow
long. Bang, bang, bang.* Instantly the magic worked.

Imagine everyone's dismay when they saw how her beauty had been changed. Her father summoned doctors and wise men to see what could be done, but it came to nothing.

At that moment of despair, Gengoroh's friend arrived at the merchant's house disguised as a priest. He mumbled certain prayers and performed a strange ceremony. Then turning to the girl's father, he said with great dignity, "This is not something a mere doctor or priest can cure. However, if you will post a notice on your gate saying that you will give a large sum of money to anyone who can cure your daughter's nose, you may have a solution to your problem."

The distraught father immediately ordered that such a sign should be put up. The curious villagers gathered round while one wise old man read the words to them. Each in turn shrugged his shoulders and walked away. There was certainly none among these simple people with the power to cure long noses.

Presently, along came Gengoroh as if by chance, innocent as the day and whistling a happy tune. He, too, read the sign and he laughed. "Well, now, I certainly could use a large sum of money," he said with a wink. "I think I'll see what I can do about the girl's nose." And as the villagers gaped, he walked boldly up to the merchant's door.

Gengoroh stated his business and the rich man gladly welcomed him into his home, even though he looked like the poorest peasant who ever worked in the rice paddies of Japan.

Gengoroh examined the nose of the young girl and shook his head sadly. "This is a very serious condition," he said. "I think I can cure her, but it can hardly be done in one day. However, let me begin the treatment now and we will see what happens."

He ordered that screens be placed about him and the girl, for, he said, the magic was so powerful that no one could watch it. Once hidden from view he tapped the drum once, very lightly, and whispered, *Nose, nose, grow short. Bang, bang, bang.* Then he allowed her to step out from behind the screen, and everyone saw that her nose was just slightly smaller.

The happy father begged Gengoroh to go on with the treatment, but the young man said he had used up all his magic for the day and would have to come back again. So the treatment continued, and by the tenth day the girl was as beautiful as she had been when she first walked into the temple garden.

The father was overjoyed and he heaped riches upon Gengoroh and his friend. The two of them built a fine house in the country and led a life of luxury and idleness. "Who would think," laughed Gengoroh, "that my simple trick would bring us such wealth."

Yet after a time this life of ease grew tiresome. One day Gengoroh came upon the drum which he had put away and forgotten about. "Dear friend Muri," he said. "Let us try the drum and see how long it can make my nose grow." He handed the drum to Muri who began tapping and saying over and over, *Gengoroh's nose, grow long. Bang, bang, bang, bang.*

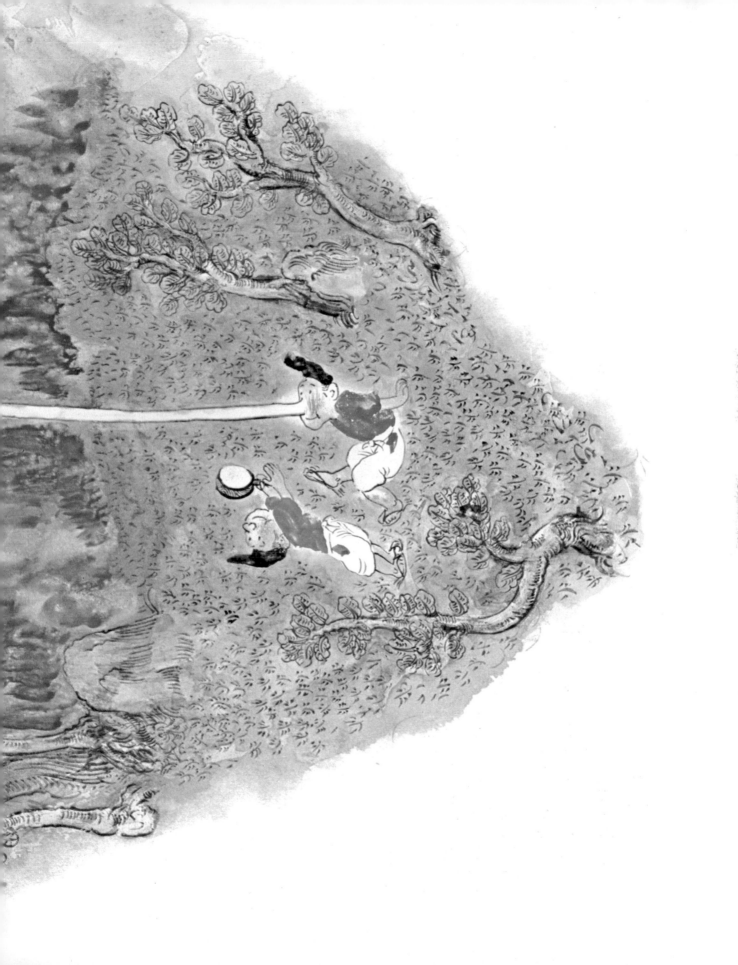

All the while the nose grew longer
and longer.

Up, up into the blue sky it went,
frightening the birds as it passed.

On and on, through a little cloud
and through a bigger cloud until
it was lost from sight.

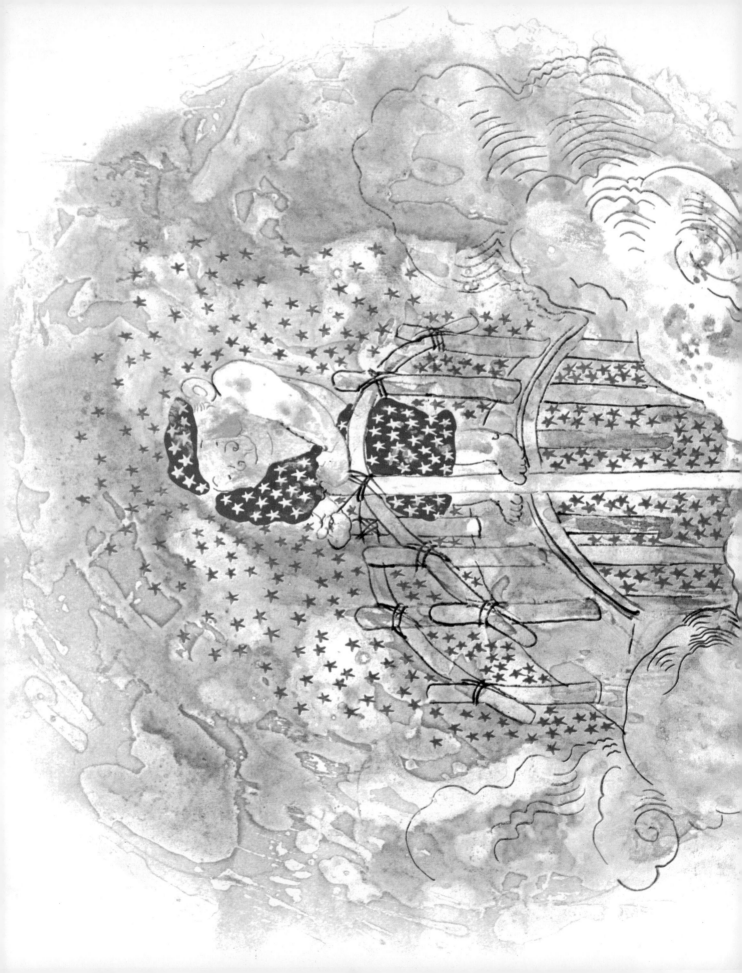

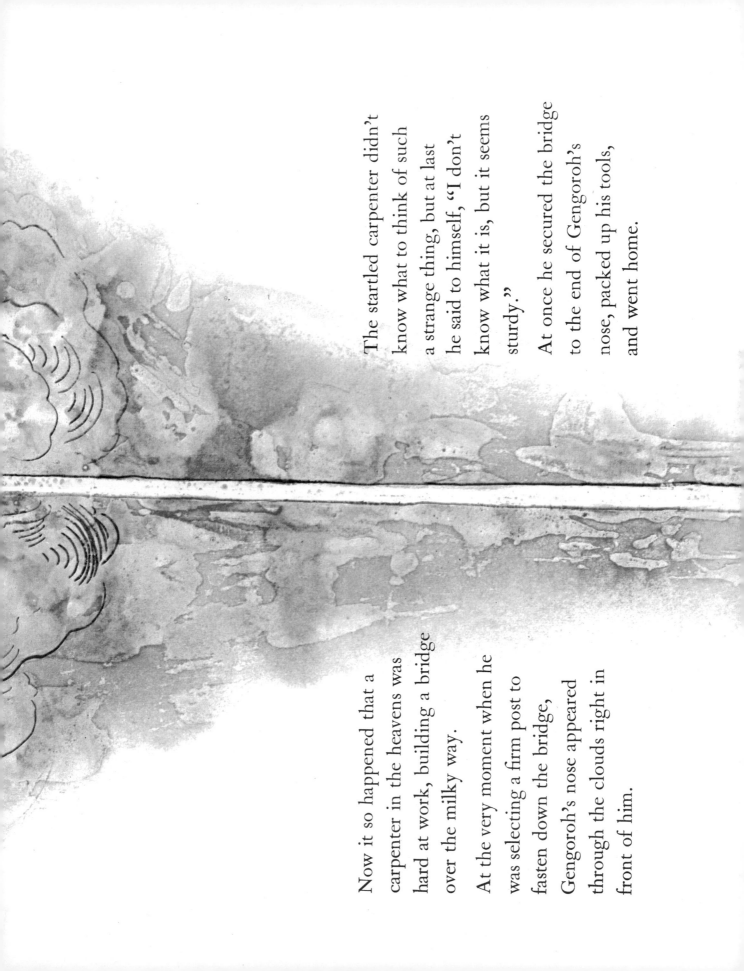

The startled carpenter didn't
know what to think of such
a strange thing, but at last
he said to himself, "I don't
know what it is, but it seems
sturdy."
At once he secured the bridge
to the end of Gengoroh's
nose, packed up his tools,
and went home.

Now it so happened that a
carpenter in the heavens was
hard at work, building a bridge
over the milky way.

At the very moment when he
was selecting a firm post to
fasten down the bridge,
Gengoroh's nose appeared
through the clouds right in
front of him.

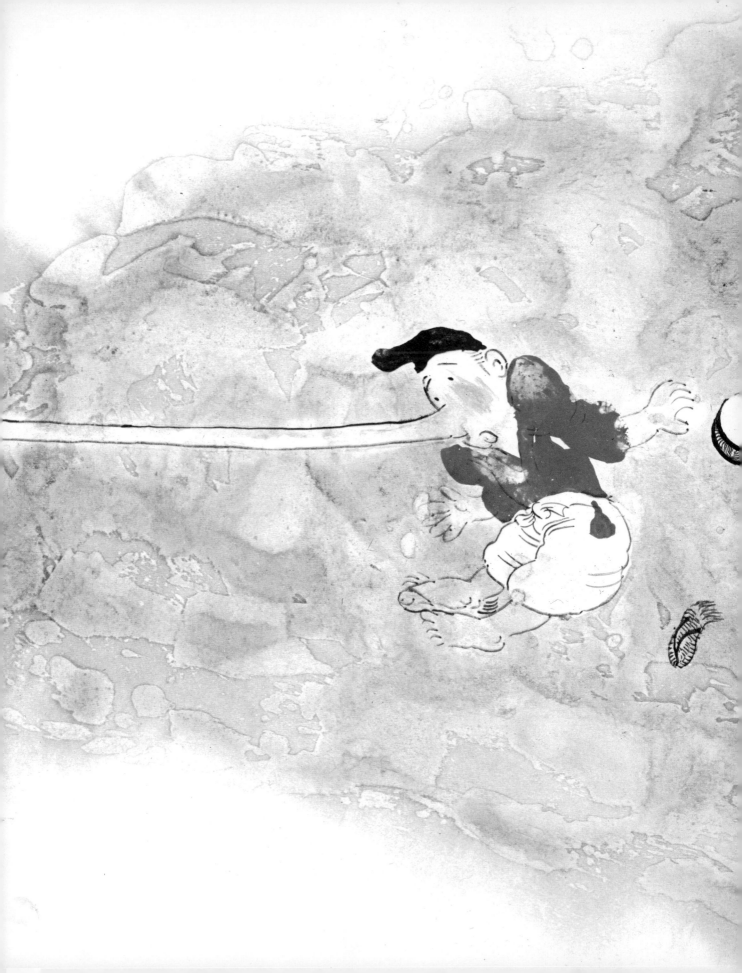

Gengoroh, of course, had no idea what was going on up there behind the clouds, but he did feel something like a tickle at the end of his nose. "Quick!" he cried to his friend. "I feel a sneeze in my nose. Make it short as fast as you can before I blow a hole in the sky!"

At once Muri began banging on the other side of the drum and shouting, *Gengoroh's nose, grow short. Bang, bang, bang!* But the carpenter had done such a good job of fastening the bridge that as Gengoroh's nose grew shorter, he was lifted up into the heavens! In his astonishment at such a sight, Muri kept right on beating the drum until his friend disappeared into the sky.

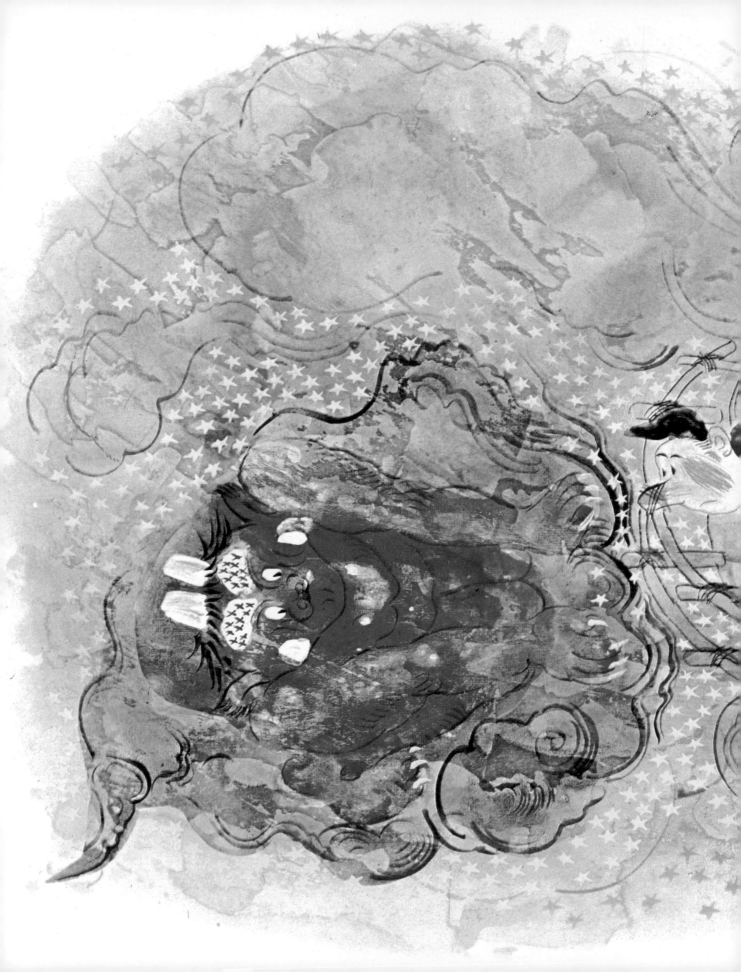

In due time Gengoroh arrived at the end of his nose, but there was nothing he could do to free himself. And if I should, he thought, I would simply fall straight down to earth and be killed. So at the top of his voice he began shouting for help in the hope that some god or another would pass by and save him.

Presently the thunder god, hearing the cries, came along to see what the trouble was. "Aha!" he cried when he saw Gengoroh. "Just who I need to be my helper." He stomped onto the bridge and untied the trembling man, taking care not to drop him.

"Thank you for saving my life," said Gengoroh, rubbing the end of his sore nose. "Now I must get back to my home on earth."

The thunder god laughed and the bridge shook under their feet. "I have much better plans for you," he said. "Stay here and be my helper. I'm sure you'll find it more exciting than anything you can do down there." With that, he began showing Gengoroh how to make storms. "This is the rake you use to gather together the clouds. This watering can holds enough water to wash all the islands of Japan into the sea, so be careful how you use it. And when you shake this mirror, the lightning flashes across the sky. These tools are for you to work with," he added. "But the thunder is so powerful that I am the only one who can handle it."

It didn't take Gengoroh long to decide that helping the thunder god was much better than living in idleness on earth.

He soon learned how to rake the clouds just right so that there would be enough rain to make the farmers' crops grow. He could make spring rains and summer storms, and the cold rains of autumn. He was careful not to make the clouds too thick, for then the rains would bring floods. And because he never forgot to do his job, the land never suffered from drought. It was most exciting when he shook the mirror and bright lightning jumped from cloud to cloud. Then the god worked his thunder machine and the earth shook with its mighty noise.

But Gengoroh still liked to play tricks. On a bright,
sunny day, when everyone had their clothes hanging
out and their beans spread out to dry in the sunshine,
he would send a sudden afternoon shower. Then such
scurrying about there was, as the housewives rushed
to take in the laundry and the farmers dropped what
they were doing to save the beans.

On one such day, as Gengoroh skipped from cloud to cloud singing and laughing at his joke, he forgot to watch his step. He slipped off the side of a cloud, and even the thunder god wasn't quick enough to save him.

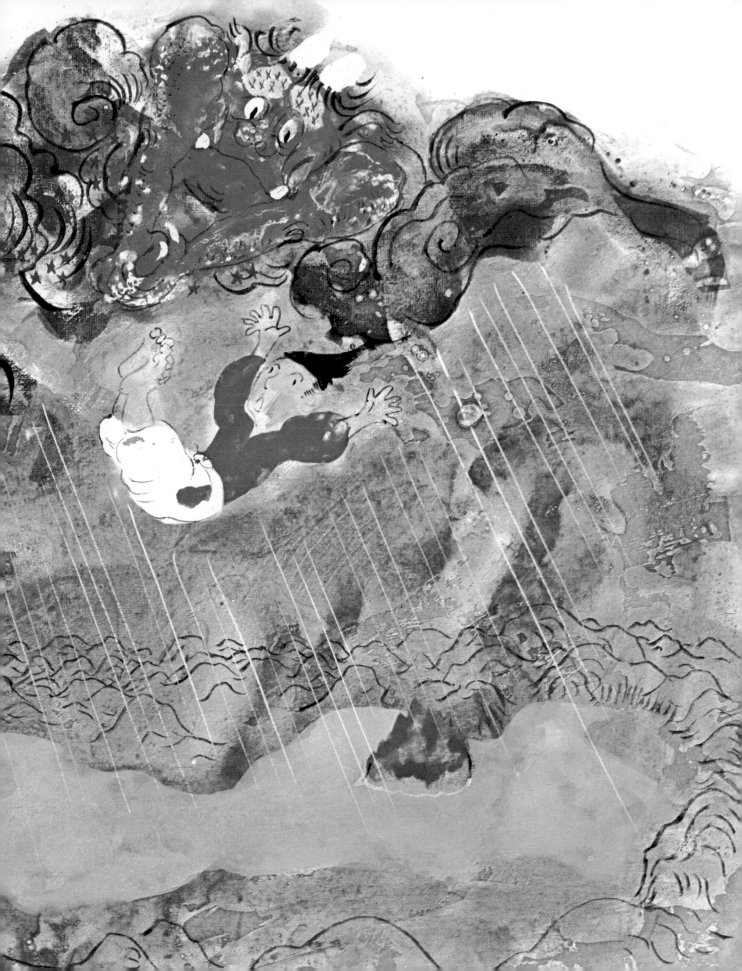

Down, down he fell, and without a doubt he would have lost his life,
but the thunder god, seeing that Gengoroh was heading for a large
lake, quickly changed him into a silvery carp. With a great splash
Gengoroh dropped into the middle of the lake where he lives to this day.
Still, from time to time as he swims about enjoying the life of a fish, he
remembers the days when he was the helper of the thunder god in heaven.